MR. MEN
ADVENTURE WITH
SUPERHEROES

Roger Hargreaves

Original concept by
Roger Hargreaves

Written and illustrated by
Adam Hargreaves

Mr Strong, as his name would suggest, was very strong. Strong by name and strong by nature. He was so strong that he did not know his own strength. Which was a problem.

It was a problem when he worked as a postman. He kept breaking postboxes.

It was a problem when he worked as a builder. He kept bending hammers.

And it was a problem when he worked as a cook. He kept snapping ladles.

Mr Strong wanted to find a job that would suit his incredible strength.

And then he had the perfect idea.

He became a superhero.

STRONGMAN

As strong as an ox.

As strong as steel.

As strong as strong cheddar.

In no time at all, he had everything ready to start his new job. There was just one thing missing. He needed a sidekick.

So Mr Strong advertised for a sidekick in the local newspaper.

A lot of people applied for the job.

Well, it's not every day you get the chance to work alongside a superhero!

Mr Strong decided to show his
first applicant around.

His house looked very normal from
the outside.

However, it was far from normal. It had
a secret staircase. A secret staircase that led
down to his superhero hideout.

Which he called The Cape Cave.

"Why is it called The Cape Cave?" asked Little Miss Curious.

"Because it's where I keep all my capes," answered Mr Strong.

"Why do you wear a cape?" asked Little Miss Curious.

"Because superheroes wear capes," answered Mr Strong.

"What makes you a superhero?" asked Little Miss Curious.

"My superpowers," answered Mr Strong, deciding that Little Miss Curious would not make a good sidekick.

There were far too many questions. Too many questions to be able to get any superhero work done.

Mr Strong proudly showed the next applicants all the gadgets in The Cape Cave. There were gadgets galore. Mr Strong was especially proud of his invisibility ray gun.

Little Miss Shy used the invisibility ray gun to make herself disappear when she was embarrassed.

Little Miss Naughty used it to stop her getting caught when she was being naughty.

SPLAT!

"You must remember that these gadgets are for stopping crime and rescuing people," explained Mr Strong, deciding that neither Little Miss Shy nor Little Miss Naughty were suitable sidekick material.

The best gadget of all was Mr Strong's Strongmobile.

But Mr Clumsy was not the man to drive it!

In fact, Mr Strong was quickly coming to realise that a lot of the applicants were not right for the job.

Mr Muddle put the superhero cape on the wrong way round.

The tights were too short for Mr Tall.

And Mr Silly wore the mask on his nose.

And then there were the superpowers.

Mr Nosey liked having X-ray vision. You can be very nosey if you can see through walls!

But this was not the sort of use that Mr Strong had in mind for X-ray vision.

Mr Greedy liked being able to fly. He could visit all the restaurants in town as quick as a flash.

"Is it a bird? Is it a balloon? Is it a flying pink blancmange? No! It's Mr Greedy!"

Mr Rude could be very rude at times!

And we won't mention Mr Rude's superpower!

PARP!

Mr Bump discovered that being a superhero did not stop him bumping into things.

The bumps just got bigger!

And poor Mr Sneeze discovered that his sneezes also just got bigger.

Mr Strong had a lot of explaining to do!

Mr Strong needed someone dynamic.

But Mr Lazy was as far from dynamic as you could get.

They would not make a dynamic duo.

When the siren went off, it was not so much
Go! **Go!** **Go!** as **Snore!** **Snore!** **Snore!**

Mr Wrong brought the wrong utility belt.

But Mr Forgetful was worse. He forgot his utility belt altogether!

When he got to the scene of the bank robbery, he did not have any superhero gadgets to catch the robbers.

Mr Tickle was even worse. He was worse than worse.

He was downright dangerous!

At the end of the week Mr Strong had seen a very long list of applicants.

And he was no closer to finding a sidekick.

He only had one more applicant to see.

Mr Impossible!

Mr Strong could not believe his luck. Mr Impossible was a natural superhero.

He could walk up the side of a building.

He could hear a
cry for help from a
thousand miles away.

He could even
get changed in a
telephone box.

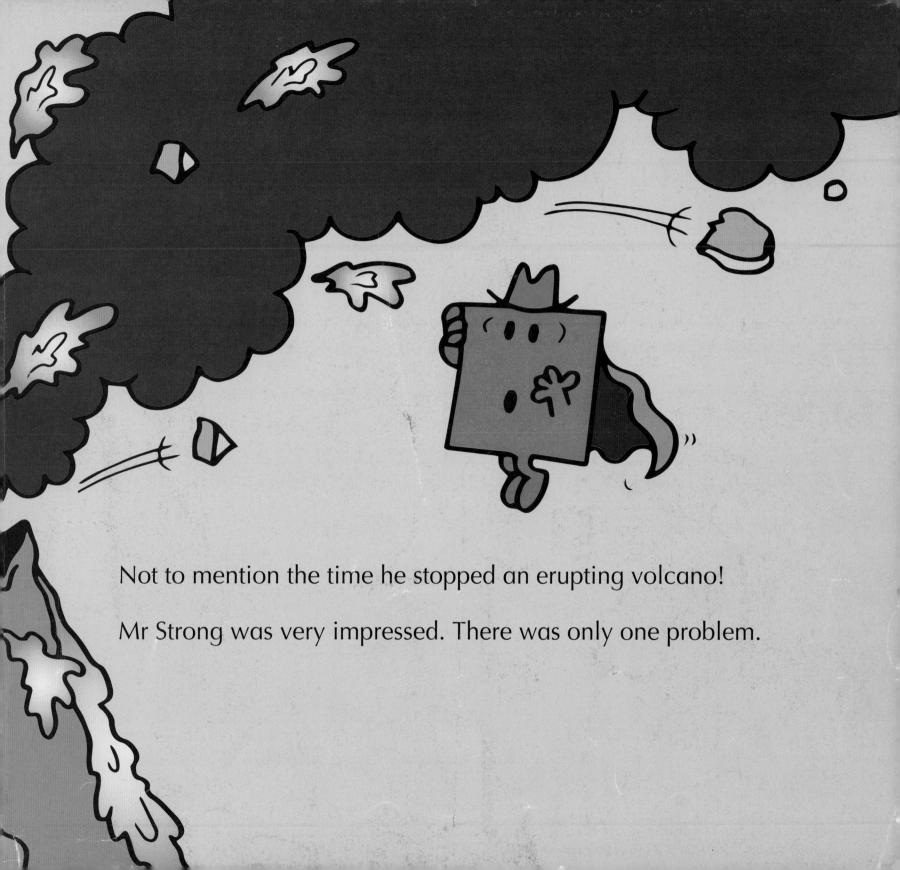

Not to mention the time he stopped an erupting volcano!

Mr Strong was very impressed. There was only one problem.

Mr Impossible was too good a superhero. Mr Strong was jealous.

Now, he felt like he was the sidekick!